Many S[hoes] Too Many To Choose!

Written and Illustrated by
Lawrence Engerman Jr.

Scan this nametag on Instagram to follow **hiphop_and_friends**.

HIP HOP & FRIENDS

Written and Illustrated by
Lawrence Gigeman Jr.

Many Shoes, Too Many To Choose!

To Elia and Emyah
My Beautiful Girls

EL

I have many shoes. My closet is full!

I have blue shoes, green shoes,
rainbow shoes too.

I have many, many shoes but not red.

I have orange instead!

Do you have shoes?

Yes, I have many!
I have every size. There are plenty.

I have big shoes and long shoes.

I have shoes that don't fit.

Some shoes are too small...

...some tall, and some zip!

I have many,
many shoes!
I can't
wear them all.

My room is filled with shoes!

I have shoes
on the wall.

Well, I have shoes with gold buckles

and some that strap!

I have some with silver that tap!

My shoes glow when I walk!

My shoes can talk!

23

Oh yeah, then what do they say?

Walk this way!

Ok, I have shoes with wings that fly.

Why lie? Good bye!

No, wait! I do have many, many shoes!

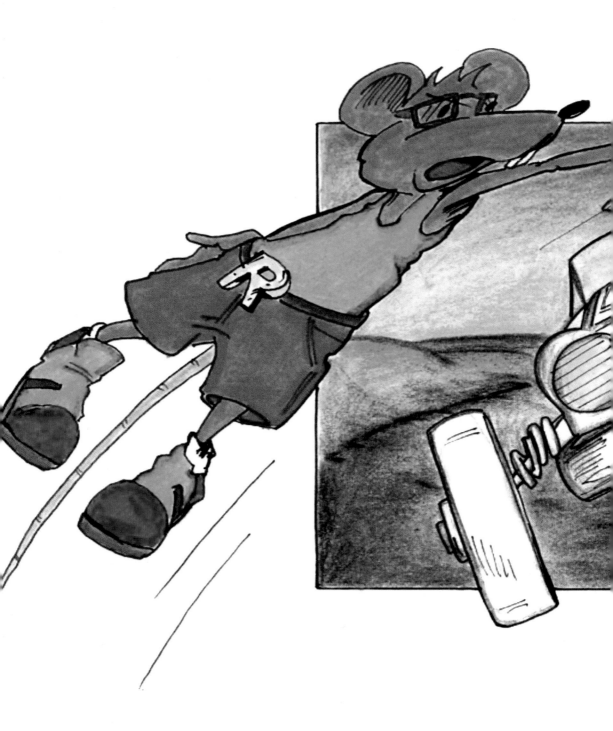

Come and see, and I will give you my many shoes, if you have more than me.

You may count my shoes
if it takes all day.
You may count fast or slow,
whichever way!

I will gladly count your shoes.
I won't stop till I'm done!

If you have even one pair less than me,
I will leave you with none!

My, my, you have many shoes indeed.

I counted and counted to 103!

I told you I have many shoes!

But not more than me!

How many do you have, 104?

I have the ones you don't see, plus more.

I will take your many, many shoes now.
I won't leave you a pair.

I'll take the new ones
    and old ones,
the shoes with a tear.

I'll take the shoes off your feet.
Those are the last.

51

I will take your many, many shoes
and laugh!

How does it feel now to have none?
Not one!

I feel sad.
I can't run.

I can't jump or kick.
I can't hop or skip.

Like yours were, my feet are bare.
Oh please may I have just one pair?

Why not?
I have many, many shoes,
green shoes and blue shoes,
too many to choose.

The truth is, I need just but one.
So take back your many shoes.
I really had none.

I'm more than happy, with just this pair.
I can run now!
My feet aren't bare.

HIP HOPS QUOTABLE

The moral of the story is don't boast or brag

About all the things that you might have

What you have some wish they had

Some live sad and some live glad

So if you are one of the fortunate few

Giving is the thing to do

And it doesn't matter how big or small

Just be grateful for it all

I CAN READ
Beginner Books